St. Patrick's Day in the Morning

St. Patrick's Day in the Morning

by Eve Bunting
illustrations by Jan Brett

Clarion Books
New York

To Debbie and Sloan, with love

Clarion Books
a Houghton Mifflin Company imprint
215 Park Avenue South, New York, NY 10003
Text copyright © 1980 by Eve Bunting
Pictures copyright © 1980 by Jan Brett Studio, Inc.
Printed in the USA

Library of Congress Cataloging in Publication Data

Bunting, Anne Eve.   St. Patrick's Day in the morning
Summary: Jamie seeks a way to prove he is not too young
to march in the big St. Patrick's Day parade.
[1. St. Patrick's Day—Fiction. 2. Parades—Fiction] I. Brett, J .n, 1949-   II. Title.
PZ7.B91527Sai [E]   79-15934   ISBN 0-395-29098-8   Paperback ISBN 0-89919-162-2

WOZ 20 19 18 17 16 15

J amie wakened early and remembered that it was St. Patrick's Day.
He climbed carefully over his big brother, Kevin, and his bigger brother, Sean.

The stairs were cold on his bare feet.

The kitchen was cold too, the fireplace full of dead ashes, like chalk.

Nell, the sheepdog, lay in the rocker.

"Here, Nell!" Jamie tried to snap his fingers the way Sean did.

Nell uncurled herself from the cushions. Jamie sat in the warm spot where she'd slept.

St. Patrick's Day in the morning. The green sashes were laid out on the table. The big one was his dad's. The next biggest was Sean's. The next biggest was Kevin's. Their fringes were crusted with gold. There was no sash for Jamie.

"It's not fair, Nell," Jamie said. "I want to walk in the parade too. They say I'm too small. That I couldn't get to the top of Acorn Hill. But what do *they* know?"

Jamie slid off the chair. His mother's raincoat hung behind the door. He put it on. He put on his dad's black hat and Sean's sash. He took Kevin's flute from the dresser.

"Come on, Nell," Jamie said.

Outside, the mountains were as green as cats' eyes. Clouds hung in tatters around their tops.

"Head up. Chest out," Jamie said. "Follow me."

They marched down the street. None of the chimneys was smoking yet. Milk bottles stood on front steps, waiting to be let in.

Kit Kelly's donkey put her head over her gate.

"A happy St. Pat's to you, donkey dear," Jamie said. He lifted his hat the way his dad did to the ladies.

Kit Kelly's donkey curled her lip.

"Silly donkey," Jamie said. "What do *you* know?"

The sky was the color of his mother's pearl brooch. The one she wore on Sundays.

Jamie marched down the middle of Main Street, past the shuttered shops.

Barney the Baker was a white blur behind his window. There was a whiff of bread baking. Nell turned her head toward the smell and drooled.

"Come on, Nell," Jamie said.

Hubble the Hen Man trundled his wheelbarrow along the footpath. His eggs were piled in it, all brown and white.

"Good morning to you," Jamie said. "I see your hens are laying well."

"It's the sweet corn and the sweet talk I feed them," Hubble said. "Pick yourself an egg, Jamie."

Jamie took a brown one off the top. It was still warm from the hen.

"Happy St. Pat's," Jamie said and lifted his hat. He put the egg safe in his pocket.

Jamie and Nell walked under the arches that spanned the street. Jamie wet the end of the flute with spit like Kevin did. Then he blew on it, and oh! the sounds he made. He puffed his cheeks. His fingers danced across the wind holes.

Nell howled and put her tail down. Silly Nell! And what did *she* know?

Mad old Mrs. Mulligan threw open her window and leaned out. "Save us all," she yelled. "It's the terrible noise you're making, Jamie Donovan." She banged her window shut.

That mad old Mrs. Mulligan! And what did *she* know?

Mrs. Mulligan's big red rooster cock-a-doodled from the roof. His wattle rattled and Nell howled again. It was as good as a chorus to go with the music. Jamie was sorry there was no one to hear but mad old Mrs. Mulligan.

It was hard climbing up Acorn Hill with all Jamie's breath
going into the music. He'd better save his strength for the
marching. He put the flute over his shoulder and stepped out.

Mrs. Simms of the Half-Way-Up Sweetshop leaned on her
half door.

"You're the early ones," she said. "Come on in, Jamie. You
likely could use some refreshments."

Jamie's head came to the level of Mrs. Simms' counter.
Bottles of ginger ale stood on it. When he looked through them
everything was orange. Mrs. Simms gave him a bottle all for
himself. She gave him a bun with a cherry on the top, too.

Nell let her tongue hang out and begged nicely. Mrs. Simms
threw her two jelly beans.

Jamie ate his bun. He put the ginger ale bottle in his other
pocket. The one that wasn't carrying the egg.

"Here's a wee flag for you, too," Mrs. Simms said. "You can wave it later on. At the parade."

Jamie sniffed. Mrs. Simms was nice. But what did *she* know? Wasn't this the parade, this very minute, and him in it? He took the flag anyway.

"We'll have to be getting on, Mrs. Simms," he said. "We've a brave bit still to go."

"Aye," Mrs. Simms said. "You'll be saving a good place for yourselves. For the watching."

Jamie nodded. "Come on, Nell."

The flute was getting awful heavy on Jamie's shoulder. He held the flag out in front of him. It was a very small flag, but it felt heavy too.

"Don't be giving up now, Nell," Jamie puffed. "We're nearly there."

They turned the sweep of Acorn hill and they *were* there.
Jamie stopped. "Look, Nell."

In front of them was the field where the bands would be and the stage for the Irish dancing. There was a green ribbon around the platform to keep the people off. Jamie crept under it. He sat right in the middle of the stage and Nell lay beside him.

The sun was coming up.

Jamie took the cap off his ginger ale and drank. He poured some in his hand for Nell.

"And all of them were saying I was too small," he said. "What do *they* know?"

The sun jumped up like a firecracker from behind the mountain.

"A happy St. Pat's to you, sun," Jamie shouted. The words made a great shimmer of sound in the emptiness.

Jamie pushed Nell's head from his knees and stood up. The last drop of ginger ale was gone from the bottle. He stuck the green and yellow flag in it. Then he put the bottle right in the middle of the stage.

"See?" he told Nell. "That means we were here first. We did it, no matter what they said. Now we can go on home."

It was easy going down Acorn Hill. There was nothing to it at all.

The town was waking up. Some of the chimneys were smoking. The milk bottles had been let in. But Jamie's own house was still asleep.

He opened the back door. The clock tick-tocked.
The turf ashes lay in their white drifts.

Jamie took off his mother's coat. He set Hubble's egg
on the table.

He climbed in the rocker and Nell jumped beside
him. He laid the flute across his knees and closed his
eyes. Oh, the music he'd made. They'd not hear the likes
of it all day. And wait till they saw the flag! The mystery
of it. The wondering there'd be.

There were feet coming down the stairs but his eyes
were too heavy to lift and look.

"Och, our Jamie!" Kevin's voice was soft. "Sound
asleep, and with the sash and the flute and our dad's
black hat. Are you sad now, and you not big enough to
walk in the parade?"

Jamie kept his eyes closed and smiled.
Silly Kevin! And what did *he* know?